Winter
A·C·R·O·S·S
AMERICA

SEYMOUR SIMON

HYPERION BOOKS FOR CHILDREN
NEW YORK

To Robert Simon and Nicole Fauteux,
and their son, my grandson,
Joel Fauteux Simon

PHOTO CREDITS

Front jacket © Stan Osolinski/Dembinsky Photo Associates; back jacket,
pp. 10–11, 23, and 32 © Seymour Simon; pp. 1, 2–3, and 5 © Gary
Braasch; pp. 6–7 © Art Wolfe; p. 8 © Frank S. Balthis; p. 13 © Scott T.
Smith; pp. 14–15 © Willard Clay/Dembinsky Photo Associates; pp. 16–
17 © Steven C. Wilson/Entheos; p. 18 © Rod Planck/Dembinsky Photo
Associates; p. 19 © George E. Stewart/Dembinsky Photo Associates; pp.
20–21, 28–29 © R. Hamilton Smith; pp. 25 and 31 © Ted Levin; p. 26 ©
Skip Moody/Dembinsky Photo Associates.

Library of Congress Cataloging-in-Publication Data

Simon, Seymour.
Winter across America/Seymour Simon
p.   cm.
ISBN 0-7868-0019-4 (trade)—ISBN 0-7868-2015-2 (lib. bdg.)
1. Winter—North America—Juvenile literature.   2. North America—
Climate—Juvenile literature.   [1. Winter—North America.
2. North America—Climate.]   I. Title.
QB637.8.S56 1994
508.7—dc20   93-45933   CIP   AC

Winter is both an ending and a beginning. It is the only season that spreads over the last days of one year and the first months of the next. Winter begins officially on or about December 21. On that day, called the winter solstice, the Northern Hemisphere slants farthest away from the sun. Fewer warming rays reach America and other countries in the North. Trees and grasses, rocks and soil, and rivers and lakes give up their heat, and the air grows colder.

Winter is a time of earth sounds: the creaking of bare trees blowing in the chill wind, the howling of a blizzard, the crunch of snow underfoot. It is a season in which seeds, insect eggs, and cocoons remain protected against the cold until the warmth of spring allows them to sprout or hatch.

Winter across America means gray whales migrating along a rainy Pacific Coast, fierce winds and the baying of coyotes in the deserts of the Southwest, ice storms and frozen beaver ponds in the Midwest, warm days and wintering geese along the Gulf Coast, and blizzards and deer tracks in the forests of the Northeast. Winter is the harshest season of the year, a testing time for animals and plants. Yet winter is also a season of hope—the promise of a new year and a new beginning.

Darkness falls quickly on the winter solstice, the shortest day of the year. In the northern states and in Alaska and Canada, there are only a few hours of pale light between sunrise and sunset. At the Arctic Circle, the sun never rises at all on the first day of winter. Between the Arctic Circle and the North Pole, the sun may not rise above the horizon for weeks or even months.

In Alaska winter comes early, with snow covering the ground by October or early November and lasting until late spring. The Inuit people of the Far North live with snow for most of the year. They use dozens of names to describe the different kinds. Here are just a few: *anniu* is falling snow, *api* is ground snow, *upsik* is wind-driven snow, *qali* is snow on the branches of trees, and *kimoaqtruk* is a snowdrift.

Some furred animals are active all winter in the snow and frigid temperatures of the North. The shaggy musk ox is well protected by a thick growth of wool beneath a heavy outer covering of hair that serves as a warm double blanket. The musk ox is not really an ox but rather a kind of giant goat. Food is scarce in winter, and the ox digs beneath the snow to search for mosses and dead grasses to eat. Musk oxen protect themselves and their young by traveling in a herd and forming a defensive line or circle against their enemies.

Farther south along the Pacific Coast, early winter days are short but the weather is mild. During the past few months, thousands of gray whales have traveled south along the coast, migrating from their feeding grounds in the cold waters of Alaska to the warm bay waters of Baja California. In early winter, many of the females give birth to calves in Baja. In January and February, the gray whales begin their journey back to the Arctic.

Gray whales are huge animals. They reach a length of forty-five feet, as long as a bus, and a weight of thirty tons, as heavy as ten elephants. They spend most of their time below the water, surfacing every few minutes to take a breath and then disappearing into the depths again. Gray whales feed along the ocean bottom, blowing water out of their mouths, stirring up the sediment, and then sucking up the cloudy water with any living things that happen to be in it. The whale surfaces every few minutes to rinse its mouth and swallow the catch.

Gray whales are dark, sometimes almost black. But their bodies are often covered by patches of white barnacles that make the whales appear gray. The photo shows a gray whale calf resting on its mother's back in California waters on its return trip to Arctic waters. The ten-thousand-mile round-trip journey of the gray whale is the longest migration of any mammal.

The Rocky Mountains, along with the Sierra Nevada, Cascade, and Coast mountain ranges, form a barrier running north to south in western America from Alaska to Mexico. Some of the highest mountains, such as Mount McKinley in Alaska, Mount Olympus and Mount Rainier in Washington, Mount Hood in Oregon, and Mount Whitney in California, are covered by ice glaciers or snow all year-round.

The westward-facing slopes of Pacific mountain ranges are wetter and snowier than the eastern slopes. That's because the prevailing winds blow from west to east, and moist air from the Pacific Ocean is forced to rise over the mountains. As the air rises, the moisture cools and condenses into clouds, which cool further as they continue rising. The moisture then falls as rain or snow. The western slopes of the Sierra Nevadas (shown here) receive as much as thirty to fifty feet of snow each winter.

The timberline on mountains is the line above which trees cannot grow. In the Sierras and southern Rockies, the timberline is about eleven thousand feet, whereas to the colder north near the Canadian border it is only seventy-five hundred feet. Above the timberline is a zone called the alpine tundra, where only flattened shrubs, mosses, and lichens can grow and few animals are found.

The North American deserts that cover much of the southwestern United States, such as the Mojave, the Sonoran, and the Great Basin, are caused by the "rain shadows" of the Pacific Coastal mountains.

Because most of the moisture falls on the upwind slopes of the mountains, a dry area called the "rain shadow" covers the down-wind side and the land to the east. Harsh, dry winds blow down the eastern slopes and across the ground, soaking up any moisture in the soil. Very little rain or snow falls.

Death Valley in the Mojave Desert is the lowest point in America, 282 feet below sea level. On the average, less than two inches of rain or snow falls a year. In the summer, the air temperature can get hotter than 130°F, but in the winter it gets cold enough for rime (a frosty or granular ice coating) to form on the Joshua trees, as shown here.

It's difficult to imagine that any plant could live with so little water and such temperature extremes, but the Joshua tree of the Mojave Desert actually thrives on the slopes of the mountains in Death Valley National Monument. The Joshua is an odd-looking kind of treelike yucca plant that may live for hundreds of years and grow to a height of twenty-five feet. It lives only in deserts where summers are scorching and winters cold. The Joshua tree needs a cold winter season during which to lie inactive before it can grow again in the spring.

The Grand Canyon of the Colorado River snakes for more than two hundred miles through northwest Arizona. It is a strange and beautiful mixture of a winding river, dry deserts, and evergreen forests set among multicolored layers of rocks, magnificent cliffs, and shelves.

Summer rains and winter snows support pinyon pines and junipers on the rim of the canyon, while the canyon walls below are dry deserts. Big pines, spruces, and firs grow above the rim in the surrounding hills. The highest spots above the rim are eight thousand feet in elevation and may get as much as ten feet of snow during the winter. To the east of the Grand Canyon, snowfall lessens and true desert appears.

The Grand Canyon is an ancient desert that was heaved above sea level many years ago to become a high, flat land called a plateau. Over time, the Colorado River scoured its way downward through layer after layer of rock to make a deep, twisting canyon. Walking the trails that wind from the floor is like a time trip into the past. Rocks in the canyon walls reveal a record of more than two million years of geologic history, with the youngest rocks located higher up and the oldest at the bottom.

Snow geese that spend spring and summer in the Arctic gather in huge numbers at winter feeding grounds such as Bosque del Apache National Wildlife Refuge in New Mexico. Small seed-eating birds that live in northern areas can usually find food even during the winter and may stay year-round. But larger birds that eat fish or water plants can't get food because northern lakes and wetlands freeze over. So several hundred different kinds of birds migrate to milder climates farther south every winter.

The seasonal journeys of North American birds involve thousands of millions of individual birds. Almost every kind has its own schedule and path, but there are four main routes: the Atlantic, the Mississippi, the Central, and the Pacific flyways. The Mississippi flyway has its beginnings in northwestern Canada. The birds move south across central Canada and then down the valley of the Mississippi River to their wintering grounds along the Gulf of Mexico.

The whooping crane, with its magnificent seven-foot wingspread, uses this route. The cranes were wildly hunted, and by 1939 only eighteen "whoopers" were left in the world. Since then, the United States and Canada have protected the whooping cranes. Still, fewer than 150 of them survive today.

Although many birds migrate to warm winter homes in the south, others are "snowbirds," which remain up north. The great gray owl lives in the forests of Canada, traveling only as far south as the northern United States when food supplies run low in winter. A mass of fluffy feathers keep this owl well protected from a snowstorm in upper Michigan. The largest of all North American owls, the great gray has a body almost three feet long. Owls have large eyes that help them do most of their hunting in the darkness, but they also depend upon their ears to locate the rustlings of mice and other rodents. An owl is so silent in flight that no sound warns its prey.

Black-capped chickadees are a common sight in the Midwest and Northeast in winter. You can easily recognize the bird by its black cap and black throat. *Chickadee* is one of the sounds it makes. Chickadees travel and feed in small flocks. They eat seeds from pine and hemlock trees and the eggs or larvae of insects and spiders that they find in cracks in the bark. Chickadees are acrobats, hanging below a snow-covered branch to feed as easily as standing atop it. Many people put out food (suet and sunflower seeds) for chicka-dees in the winter. The birds are so friendly and inquisitive that they will often pick up seeds from a person's hand.

One of the most beautiful winter storms is a glaze, or ice, storm. Glaze forms when raindrops fall through a layer of very cold air and freeze as they touch the ground. Glaze can also form when raindrops fall on a frozen surface. In either case, a thin layer of ice quickly coats roads, sidewalks, houses, bushes, trees, and telephone and power lines.

Although everything looks like a dazzling crystal world, an ice storm can be very dangerous. Roads and sidewalks turn slippery under a layer of almost invisible "black ice." Telephone and power lines become enclosed in ice casings that increase in size during the storm. When the weight of the ice becomes too great, the lines break.

Branches of trees and bushes are sometimes coated by layers of ice more than two inches thick. Branches bend and splinter under the weight, and trees break and collapse. The photo shows a forest of glittering trees in Minnesota after an ice storm.

The warm winter of the Florida Everglades doesn't seem to be the same season as the icy winter of the North. The Everglades are thousands of square miles of freshwater marshes, small ponds, and tree-covered islands, sometimes called the "river of grass." Saw grass is the main plant of the Everglades. Each blade of saw grass has a row of sharp teeth on both edges and another down the middle. In winter, the saw grass dies and the blades fall and decay, adding to the wetland bottom.

The anhinga is a common fish-eating bird of the Everglades. It often swims with just its head showing above the water and is sometimes called a snake bird because of the snakelike curve of its head and neck. After the anhinga (an-HIN-ga) catches a fish in its beak, it spins the fish around and swallows it whole. There are hundreds of different species of birds that live in the Everglades year-round, and winter brings large numbers of waterfowl and shorebirds from the North.

Many other animals also live in the Everglades area and are active during the mild winters. Raccoons, black bears, and white-tailed deer live among the swamps and marshes. Alligators, otters, snakes, turtles, and frogs swim in the water holes and come out to sun themselves. Insects, including mosquitoes and hosts of butterflies, are also active in the winter.

In cold northern regions, the water in ponds and lakes freezes into ice crystals from the surface downward. The ice is usually not solid down to the bottom unless the pond or lake is very shallow. The layer of ice on top acts as a protective covering below which many plants and animals can survive the cold of winter. When the pond water turns cold, turtles, frogs, salamanders, and other cold-blooded water animals burrow into the mud at the bottom of a pond or lake, where they will hibernate (go into a deep sleep and remain almost lifeless) until the spring thaw.

Some of the fish, such as northern pike and brook trout, may be active all winter. Muskrats and beavers are water-dwelling mammals that remain active during the winter. Both have thick coats of waterproof fur that keep them warm. These animals build lodges in the water made of sticks, mud, and plant materials, and they also dig underground dens in the banks. The lodges usually have an entrance underwater and a chamber inside. In winter, muskrats and beavers feed on the roots of water plants.

Otters sometimes live in abandoned muskrat and beaver dens. Otter tracks, such as these by a partially frozen stream, are easy to spot. Otters travel across the snow by bounding and sliding. The slide is a wide path through the snow, starting and ending with a group of paw prints. Otters keep a hole or two open in a frozen lake so they can fish even during the winter.

Mammals that remain active during northern winters usually have some special characteristics that help them survive the cold and snow. Red and gray squirrels remain active during mild winter weather but stay in their nests when the weather turns bad. During bad weather the squirrels eat nuts and acorns they have stored in various places. Mice, voles, and some other small mammals gather in groups in nests beneath the snow and huddle together so that their body heat is lost much more slowly.

Weasels and other small mammals that do come out for short periods during the winter grow a thicker coat of fur, adding a layer of insulation. Porcupines that roam most of the year find it hard to walk in deep snow, so they feed on inner bark and the branches of trees close to their dens.

The long legs of white-tailed deer reach down through the snow cover to firm ground. But when the snow gets too deep even for them, deer pack down the snow in a network of trails within a small area called a "deer yard."

The snowshoe hare walks on top of the snow more easily, supported by the oversize feet that give it its name. The hare's brown fur changes to white in winter, making it difficult for foxes and other predators to spot against the snow. The ermine, a type of weasel, also changes to a white winter coat that makes it difficult to be seen by the small animals upon which it feeds.

The biggest winter storms are called blizzards. The weather bureau calls a storm a blizzard if snow falls for a long period of time, winds blow stronger than thirty-five miles per hour, and the visibility is one-quarter of a mile or less. Some blizzards are much worse than that.

Giant winter blizzards often begin with a storm from the Pacific Ocean hitting the West Coast. The storm usually starts as rain when it comes ashore. As the storm moves inland, the rain turns to snow over the colder Sierra Nevadas, sometimes dumping ten or fifteen feet of snow on higher elevations. With little moisture left, the storm may only dust the Rockies. Moving across the Midwest, the storm begins to draw in warm, humid air from the Gulf of Mexico and cold air from Canada. These air masses supply the moisture and energy needed for a blizzard. From the Midwest, storms follow various tracks in the Northeast or Mid-Atlantic states, sometimes kicking up "secondary" storms along the East Coast.

The end of winter comes gradually to northern lands. Birds that have traveled to southern states begin returning north. Buds on trees such as maples, poplars, and pussy willows begin to swell. The groundhog may come out of hibernation from its underground den and nose around for food. Roads and fields turn to mud as the ground thaws and ice and snow melt. Earthworms come to the surface and leave worm casings on lawns. In wetlands, skunk cabbage turns green. Early spring flowers such as snowdrops and crocuses may bloom.

In the New England states, perhaps the most welcome sign of winter's end is when sugar maple trees are tapped for syrup. On warm days in late winter, sap (a watery liquid food) begins flowing up the trunk of a tree from the roots. Many kinds of maples and birches produce sap that can be used to make syrup, but the sweetest sap comes from sugar maples. Native Americans long ago discovered that the sap could be collected and boiled down to make a thick, sweet syrup for eating.

To collect the sap, several small tubes are inserted two or three inches into the tree trunk, and buckets are hung beneath the spouts. The sap drips out slowly, and when the buckets are filled, the collected sap is boiled down to evaporate the water and thicken the liquid. It takes between twenty and forty gallons of sap to make one gallon of maple syrup.

Winter is falling snows and nights falling fast. It is the sound of the wind blowing through the dark shapes of leafless trees out-lined against the white ground. It is a film of ice needles on a pond or stream. It is the silence of glittering stars on a frosty night. Winter brings rest and renewal. It is a pause in the great, eternal cycle of the seasons.